Brail

Thank You Bear

Thank You Bear

by Greg Foley

SCHOLASTIC INC.
New York Toronto London Auckland
Sydney Mexico City New Delhi Hong Kong

For anyone who ever thought they had something great.

Early one morning,
a little bear found a little box.

He looked inside and said,
"Why, it's the greatest thing ever!
Mouse will love this."

On his way to find Mouse,
he showed it to the monkey.
Monkey said,
"That's not so great."

He showed it to the owl.
Owl said,
"I've seen those before."

He showed it to the fox.
Fox said,
"You're holding it the wrong way."

He showed it to the elephant.
Elephant said,
"I think it's too small."

He showed it to the squirrel.
Squirrel said,
"It would be much better
if you gave it to me."

He tried to show it to the bunny.
But Bunny said,
"I don't have time to look right now."

The little bear stopped.
He wondered whether
it was so great after all.

While he was wondering,
Mouse came along
and asked Bear what he had.

He put the box on the ground
and showed it to Mouse.
Mouse looked at it this way and that.

Then Mouse crawled inside
the empty box and said,
"It's the greatest thing ever!"

"Thank you, Bear."

ISBN: 978-0-545-22945-6

12 11 10 9 8 7 6 5 4 3 2 1   10 11 12 13 14 15/0

Printed in Singapore   46

First Scholastic printing, January 2010

Set in American Typewriter Regular